All Wet! All Wet!

ALL WET! ALL WET!

by James Skofield

Illustrated by Diane Stanley

Harper & Row, Publishers

Library of Congress Cataloging in Publication Data
Skofield, James.
    All wet! All wet!

    "A Charlotte Zolotow book."
    Summary: A small boy experiences, along with
the animals of meadow and forest, the sights,
smells, and sounds of a rainy summer day.
    [1. Rain and rainfall—Fiction.   2. Forest
animals—Fiction.   3. Meadow animals—Fiction]
I. Stanley, Diane, ill.   II. Title.
PZ7.S62835Al 1984   [E]   82-47713
ISBN 0-06-025751-2
ISBN 0-06-025752-0 (lib. bdg.)

For Jan Aldrich
and Charlotte Zolotow
between whom flourishes
an alphabet

J.S.

For Cleo and Faye,
who could brighten
any rainy day.

D.S.

The rain begins at dawn.
It stirs the leaves on quiet trees.
It drifts across the sleeping meadow.

Up in the woods, a mother fox
scents the dampening breeze and goes to earth.

The rabbits snuggle in their burrow;
they listen to the whispering rain.

In the stream, the silent fish
hear the sound of the rain upon their roof.

And in the wood, a quail calls,
"All wet! All wet!"

The rainy day begins.

Inside a hollow log, Skunk wakes and yawns,
then steps outside and ambles toward the stream.
Skunk passes spiders, sitting like black stars,
motionless, at the hub of diamond webs.

He steps around the tiny, gold-red mushrooms
and comes upon Quail's unprotected nest.
Skunk snatches up an egg and shuffles on.

High above, three noisy rain crows shriek
"Wet skunk! Egg thief! Too bad!"

But Skunk ignores the rain crows' scolding taunts;
he sits down by the stream to eat his egg.

Across from him, the rain falls on two deer
who bend to drink, then . . . pause . . . then drink again.

Skunk finishes his egg. He sniffs and drinks
and grouches off back to his hollow log.
A river hawk dives soundlessly for fish.
By noon, the rain becomes a steady pour
which flattens meadow grass in tangled clumps.

Below, and blind, the soft, star-nosed mole swims
through dark and damp, deep-rooted, fragrant earth.
In her warm den, the mother fox gives nurse;
in their dry burrows, rabbits dream of fox.

While Quail clucks and searches for her egg,
Skunk burps and falls asleep inside his log.
Beside Skunk's log, on bristling thistle stalks,
snails leave wet trails that glisten in the rain.

Below the hill, the stream swells to a creek;
the fish lurk silently deep in the pools.
Dark clouds hang low; the thunder roars its name.
The afternoon is washed by falling rain.
Even the rain crows finally fall still;
they hunch upon a fir tree's dripping limb.

Then, as the day grows old, the storm trails off
to gentle rain...then fades...then...stops.

Enormous silence fills the breathing world;
the rain has gone from hill and field and wood.

The dark clouds roll away and light breaks through;
each blade of grass is flashing like a jewel.

Frantic gnats swarm and dance in beams of sun.
The creek shrinks to a stream; the slow fish rise....
"Rain through! Sun down! To rest!"
calls Quail as she settles on her nest.

Skunk dozes in his warm log, safe and dry, and dreams of suppertime. The deer slip by, sniffing fresh air and heading for the stream.

The star-nosed mole kicks up a run of earth
and blinks up at the sky, where one small star
blinks back at her. Beside the quiet stream,
the deer drink silently, then . . . bound away.

The tree toads tune up for their evening song,
and by their burrows, rabbits watch the moon.
Up in the woods, deep in her shadowy den,
Fox waits until her kittens sleep, and then,
she steps outside and scents the evening breeze.

She sees the silver moon rise through the trees.
Then, paw after velvet paw, she picks her way
up to the hills, where she hears, clear and quiet,
the cool, dark, green-deep voice of summer night.